MATILDA

Who told Lies,
and was
Burned to Death

other books for children
by Posy Simmonds

Fred
Lulu and The Flying Babies
The Chocolate Wedding

THIS IS A BORZOI BOOK PUBLISHED BY ALFRED A. KNOPF, INC.
Text copyright © 1991 by The Estate of Hilaire Belloc
Illustrations copyright © 1991 by Posy Simmonds
All rights reserved under International and Pan-American Copyright
Conventions. Published in the United States by Alfred A. Knopf, Inc.,
New York. Distributed by Random House, Inc., New York. Originally
published in Great Britain by Jonathan Cape Ltd. in 1991.

First American Edition, 1992

Printed in Hong Kong
2 4 6 8 0 9 7 5 3 1

Library of Congress Cataloging-in-Publication Data
Belloc, Hilaire, 1870–1953.
Matilda, who told lies, and was burned to death / Hilaire Belloc ;
Illustrated by Posy Simmonds. — 1st American ed.
p.   cm.   Summary: An incorrigible liar finds that when she
needs help the most no one will believe what she has to say.
ISBN 0-679-82658-0 (trade) — ISBN 0-679-92658-5 (lib. bdg.)
1. Children's poetry, English. [1. Behavior—Poetry.
2. Narrative poetry. 3. English poetry.] I. Simmonds, Posy, ill.
II. Title PR6003.E45M38   1992 8211.912—dc20   91-15852

Hilaire Belloc

MATILDA

Who told Lies, and was Burned to Death

Illustrated by Posy Simmonds

ALFRED A. KNOPF 🐎 NEW YORK

For Pat Kavanagh

Matilda told such Dreadful Lies,
It made one Gasp and Stretch one's Eyes;

Her Aunt, who from her earliest Youth,
Had kept a Strict Regard for Truth,
Attempted to Believe Matilda:
The effort very nearly killed her,
And would have done, had not She
Discovered this Infirmity.

For once, towards the Close of Day,
Matilda, growing tired of play,
And finding she was left alone....

Went tiptoe to the Telephone

And summoned the Immediate Aid
Of London's Noble Fire Brigade.

Within an hour the Gallant Band
Were pouring in on every hand,

From Putney, Hackney Downs and Bow,
With Courage high and Hearts a-glow
They galloped, roaring through the Town....

"Matilda's House is Burning Down!"

Inspired by British Cheers and Loud
Proceeding from the Frenzied Crowd,

They ran their ladders through a score
Of windows on the Ball Room Floor;

And took Peculiar Pains to Souse
The Pictures up and down the House,

Until Matilda's Aunt succeeded
In showing them they were not needed
And even then she had to pay
To get the Men to go away!

It happened that a few Weeks later
Her Aunt was off to the Theatre
To see that Interesting Play
The Second Mrs Tanqueray.
She had refused to take her Niece
To hear this Entertaining Piece:
A Deprivation Just and Wise
To Punish her for telling Lies.

That Night a Fire *did* break out—

You should have heard Matilda Shout!
You should have heard her Scream and Bawl,

And throw the window up and call
To People passing in the Street—
(The rapidly increasing Heat
Encouraging her to obtain
Their confidence)

— but all in vain!

For every time She shouted "Fire!"
They only answered "Little Liar!"

And therefore when her Aunt returned,
Matilda, and the House, were Burned.